S0-CJN-920

Poetry Anthology 1
Head to a Pleasant Spot
And Other Poems to Remember

Written by
Susan Blackaby

Illustrated by
Meg McLean

To the Red-tailed Readers
SB

To Emma, the best reader (and daughter) I know
MM

Susan Blackaby has worked in educational publishing for over 30 years. In addition to her writing curriculum, she is the author of *Rembrandt's Hat* (Houghton Mifflin, 2002); *Cleopatra: Egypt's Last and Greatest Queen* (Sterling, 2009); *Nest, Nook, and Cranny* (Charlesbridge, 2010), winner of the 2011 Lion and the Unicorn Award for Excellence in North American Poetry; and *Brownie Groundhog and the February Fox* (Sterling, 2011). She lives in Portland, Oregon.

Meg McLean is a children's illustrator and painter whose work has appeared in books and magazines such as *Click*, *Muse*, *Weekly Reader*, and *Zootles* as well as on countless canvases, walls, stage sets, goose eggs, and the odd piece of furniture. She earned an MFA from Cranbrook Academy of Art, where she studied painting and drawing. She now lives in Lyme, New Hampshire.

Text copyright © 2014 Susan Blackaby
Illustration copyright © 2014 Meg McLean

All Rights Reserved
No part of this book may be reproduced or transmitted in any form or by any means, electronic, mechanical, photocopying, recording, or otherwise, without prior written permission from the publisher.
For information, contact Flyleaf Publishing.

A Book to Remember™
Published by Flyleaf Publishing

For orders or information, contact us at **(800) 449-7006**.
Please visit our website at **www.flyleafpublishing.com**

Eighth Edition 2/20
Library of Congress Catalog Card Number: 2014939798
ISBN-13: 9781605411736
Printed and bound in the USA at Worzalla Publishing, Stevens Point, WI

Contents

The Batter Gets a Break

The pitcher pitched, and it was great—
A breaking ball across the plate.
The batter stepped into the swing.
The batter did not hit a thing.
Strike One.

The pitcher pitched, and it was great—
A curve ball swerved across the plate.
The batter thought, "Give me break!
I need a pitch that I can take."
Ball One.

The pitcher pitches. It is great—
A fast ball zings across the plate.
The batter swings. She breaks the bat!
The ball sails past the warning track!
Home run!

Max and Bitty Disobey

I am teaching Max and Bitty,
My black dog and my grey kitty,
A big trick. There's nothing to it!
All they've got to do is do it!
I say, "Hey! You must stand still!"
I think they can. I hope they will.
Max and Bitty disobey—
Bitty naps, Max runs away.
Max rolls over, Bitty leaps.
Max gets jumpy, Bitty sleeps.
Max and Bitty, they're so lazy!
Max and Bitty make me crazy!
They'll obey me, just you wait.
Max and Bitty will be great!

I Cannot Wait
Until I'm Eight

I cannot wait until I'm eight!
I'll be this tall, I'll be this weight.
I'll be the perfect size to ride
The Coaster Sleigh at Sunnyside.
It twirls and swirls, it zips and dips!
It dives and rocks and rolls and skips!
It holds a freight of screaming kids,
To loop the loop, to scoot and skid!
It curves and swerves in crazy eights,
Before the driver hits the brakes!
The Coaster Sleigh glides to the end
And then it starts back up again.
I cannot wait, I cannot wait,
I cannot wait until I'm eight!

SUNNYSIDE

6

Reindeer in the Far North

The reindeer herd runs swiftly
As snow falls like a veil,
It drifts across the landscape,
Craggy peak to icy dale.

The moon glows in the inky sky,
Fluffy skeins of clouds pass by.
The reindeer herd runs swiftly
On the frozen Arctic trail.

Sidney's Pet

Sidney gets to pick a pet!
Which new pet will Sidney get?
Which new pet can Sidney use?
Which new pet will Sidney choose?

A lizard has a wiggly tail,
A chimpanzee will swing.
Slugs and snails make gooey trails.
A bumblebee can sting.

Alley cats can prowl and pounce.
Turkeys gobble, joeys bounce.
Electric eels are icky slick.
Donkeys bray and like to kick.

A jersey cow will be too big.
Hens are messy, so are pigs.
But wait!
Past the guppies and the fox,
Sid sees puppies in a box.

Sleepy balls of fluffy fur—
A puppy is the pet for her.
This is the pet that Sidney picks,
And best of all, Sid picks all six!

9   Target Letter-Sound Correspondence: Long /ē/ sound spelled **ey**

Upside-Down Sheila

Sheila lives down in New Zealand,
Where the world is upside-down.
Do they dangle from the ceiling
Or do handstands on the ground?

Do they have to do things out of order—
Day is night and night is day?
Is it noon when Sheila's sleeping?
Is it midnight when she plays?

When I asked Sheila about it,
She received my note and called.
Sheila said she was not really
Hanging upside down at all.

I asked, "If you are upright
Are you snowboarding or skiing?"
Sheila laughed, and she said, "Neither!
It is summer in New Zealand!"

Either Sheila needs new glasses
Or else looks can be deceiving.
After all, it's January,
My pal Sheila must be teasing!

Head to a Pleasant Spot

When the weather is hot,
Here's a heavenly spot.
Other kids just like you
Will be heading there, too.
It's a pool!

When you've had enough sun,
You feel sweaty—No fun!
You can swim many laps
Or just drift on your back
In a pool!

Get ready, get set,
Then take a deep breath.
With your arms overhead,
You can hop off the edge
Of the pool!

Just dive in headfirst
For a fresh, pleasant burst.
You'll feel so much better!
Get wet and get wetter
In a pool.

Splish splash! You are in!
You sink up to your chin!
You felt heavy as lead?
You're a feather instead
In a pool!

Plug your nose for a dunk,
Do some handstands and jumps
Or other new tricks
With paddles and kicks
In a pool.

Use the springboard to hop
For a flip, not a flop.
Go off the deep end
And then do it again
In a pool!

When the weather is hot,
Here's a heavenly spot
Which is pleasant and fun
For kids under the sun—
It's a pool!

Brunch at Wanda's Diner

Pig called all her buddies
To invite them out to eat.
"We can meet at Wanda's Diner,
And remember—it's my treat."
All the animals were hungry
As they slid into their seats.

Koala wanted pasta
And a tall glass of iced tea.
Walrus wanted tacos
With a side of frozen peas.
Swan had enchiladas,
And the llama had grilled cheese.

Target Letter-Sound Correspondence: Short /ŏ/ sound spelled *a*

Doggy asked for waffles
And a small order of yams.
Pig said, "I am starving,
Wanda, please bring me some clams,
And I also want tamales
And a side of toast with jam."

All the critters chomped and swallowed,
All the critters ate their fill.
Then they said goodbye to Wanda,
Who stood waiting at the till—
And since Pig forgot her wallet,
Swan and Llama paid the bill.

Poetry Anthology 1 Word Lists

Prerequisite Skills

Single consonants and short vowels
Final double consonants **ff**, **gg**, **ll**, **nn**, **ss**, **tt**, **zz**
Consonant /k/ **ck**
Consonant /j/ **g**, **dge**
Consonant /s/ **c**
/ng/ **n[k]**
Consonant digraphs /ng/ **ng**, /th/ **th**, /hw/ **wh**
Consonant digraphs /ch/ **ch**, **tch**, /sh/ **sh**, /f/ **ph**
Schwa /ə/ **a, e, i, o, u**
Long /ā/ **a_e**
Long /ē/ **e_e, ee, y**
Long /ī/ **i_e, igh**
Long /ō/ **o_e**
Long /ū/, /ōo/ **u_e**
r-Controlled /ar/ **ar**
r-Controlled /or/ **or**
r-Controlled /ûr/ **er, ir, ur, ear, or, [w]or**
/ô/ **al, all**
/ul/ **le**
/d/ or /t/ **–ed**
/ou/ **ou, ow**
/ô/ **au, aw**
/oi/ **oi, oy**

Batter Gets a Break
page 1

Long /ā/ sound spelled *ea*

break
breaking
breaks
great

High-Frequency Puzzle Words

give
into
one
thought
was

Story Puzzle Word

warning

Decodable Words

a
across
and
ball
bat
batter
can
curve

did
fast
gets
he
hit
home
I
is
it
me
need
not
past
pitch
pitched
pitcher
pitches
plate
run
sails
stepped
strike
swerved
swing
swings
take
that
the
thing
track
zings

Max and Bitty Disobey
page 3

Long /ā/ sound spelled *ey*

disobey
grey
hey
obey
they
they'll
they're
they've

High-Frequency Puzzle Words

do
to
you

Story Puzzle Word

nothing

Decodable Words

a
all
am
and
away
be
big
bitty

black
can
crazy
dog
gets
got
great
hope
I
is
it
jumpy
just
kitty
lazy
leaps
make
Max
me
must
my
naps
over
rolls
runs
say
sleeps
so
stand
still
teaching

Poetry Anthology 1 Word Lists

there's
think
trick
wait
will

I Cannot Wait Until I'm Eight
page 5

Long /ā/ sound spelled *eigh*

eight
eights
freight
sleigh
weight

High-Frequency Puzzle Words

again
of
to

Decodable Words

a
and
at
back
be
before
brakes
cannot
coaster

crazy
curves
dips
dives
driver
end
glides
hits
holds
I
I'll
I'm
in
it
kids
loop
perfect
ride
rocks
rolls
scoot
screaming
size
skid
skips
starts
Sunnyside
swerves
swirls
tall
the

then
this
twirls
until
up
wait
zips

Reindeer in the Far North
page 7

Long /ā/ sound spelled *ei*

reindeer
skeins
veil

High-Frequency Puzzle Words

of
to

Decodable Words

a
across
Arctic
as
by
clouds
craggy
dale
falls
far

fluffy
frozen
glows
herd
icy
in
inky
it
landscape
like
moon
North
on
pass
peak
runs
sky
snow
swiftly
the
trail

Sidney's Pet
page 9

Long /ē/ sound spelled *ey*

alley
donkeys
gooey
jersey
joeys
Sidney
Sidney's
turkeys

Decodable Words

a
all
and
balls
are
be
best
big
but
can
for
get
gets
has
her
fur
how

in
is
like
make
new
pick
picks
sees
six
so
that
the
this
to
too
use
which
will
bounce
box
bray
bumblebee
cats
chimpanzee
choose
cow
eels
electric
fluffy
fox

18

Poetry Anthology 1 Word Lists

gobble
guppies
hens
icky
kick
lizard
messy
past
pet
pigs
pounce
prowl
puppies
puppy
Sid
sleepy
slick
slugs
snails
sting
swing
tail
trails
wait
wiggly

Upside-Down Sheila
page 11

Long /ē/ sound spelled *ei*

ceiling
deceiving
either
neither
received
Sheila
Sheila's

High-Frequency Puzzle Words

are
do
from
laughed
lives
of
said
was
where
you

Story Puzzle Words

January
skiing

Decodable Words

about
after
all
and
asked
at
be
boarding
called
can
dangle
day
down
else
glasses
ground
handstands
hanging
I
if
in
is
it
it's
looks

midnight
must
my
needs
new
night
noon
not
note
on
or
order
out
pal
plays
really
she
sleeping
snow
summer
teasing
the
they
things
upright
upside
when
world
Zealand

Head to a Pleasant Spot
page 13

Short /ĕ/ sound spelled *ea*

breath
feather
head
heading
heavenly
heavy
instead
overhead
pleasant
sweaty
weather

High-Frequency Puzzle Words

again
are
do
many
new
of
other
some
there
to

too
you
your

Story Puzzle Words

enough
pool
springboard
you'll
you're
you've

Decodable Words

a
and
arms
as
back
be
better
burst
can
chin
deep
dive
drift
dunk
edge

end
feel
felt
first
flip
flop
for
fresh
fun
get
go
had
handstands
here's
hop
hot
in
is
it
it's
jumps
just
kicks
kids
laps
lead
like
much
no

nose
not
off
on
or
paddles
plug
ready
set
sink
so
splash
splish
spot
sun
swim
take
the
then
tricks
under
up
use
wet
wetter
when
which
will
with

Brunch at Wanda's Diner
page 15

Short /ŏ/ sound spelled *a*

all
also
animals
called
enchiladas
koala
llama
pasta
small
swallowed
swan
tacos
tall
tamales
waffles
wallet
Walrus
Wanda
Wanda's
want
wanted

High-Frequency Puzzle Words

into
of
said
some
their
to
were
who

Decodable Words

a
am
an
and
as
asked
at
ate
bill
bring
brunch
buddies
but
can
cheese
chomped
clams

critters
diner
doggy
eat
extra
fill
for
forgot
frozen
glass
goodbye
grilled
had
her
hungry
I
iced
invite
it's
jam
me
meet
my
order
out
paid
peas
pig
please

remember
seats
side
since
slid
starving
stood
tea
the
them
then
they
till
treat
waiting
we
with
yams